tim the tiny horse

Harry Hill used to be a doctor but not for a long time now. He's had many TV shows and he tells jokes for a living. His hobbies are painting and drawing and occasional games of swing ball.

tim the tiny horse

by Harry Hill

ff

FABER AND FABER

For Kitty, Winnie and Freddie

First published in 2006
by Faber and Faber Limited
3 Queen Square London WCIN 3AU
This paperback edition first published in 2007

Printed in the United Kingdom by Butler and Tanner

Design and colour work by Ken de Silva

The right of Harry Hill to be identified as author of this work has been asserted in accordance with Section 77 of the Copyright, Designs and Patents Act 1988

A CIP record for this book is available from the British Library

ISBN 978-0-571-22956-7

2 4 6 8 10 9 7 5 3 1

Contents

tim and the disappearing hula hoop

Tim the Tiny Horse
was tiny...

but cheerful. Here he is
playing with a 2p piece.
so you get the idea.

A sugar lump would last
him a month.

His stable was a matchbox...

with an old tic tac box
for a conservatory.

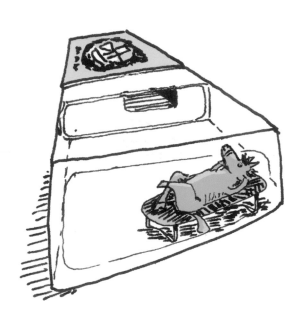

You know, somewhere
for Tim to chill out.

One fine day, Tim
the Tiny Horse went
to get his Hula Hoop
for Lunch.

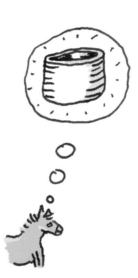

It was a barbecue flavoured one
that he'd saved from a Party.

But to his horror...
it had gone!

only a slight whiff
of barbecue sauce
lingered where once
was Tim's Hula Hoop.

Disappointed, he
wandered home,
still hungry.

Ah!

On the way, what
do you think he saw?

munch! munch!

That's right!
A fly munching into
his very own Hula Hoop!

A fight followed.

First Tim seemed to
be winning...

then the fly seemed
to gain the upper hand.

But after about a minute
they'd both had enough...

and agreed to
Share it.

Later on, they sat down
and watched a video together.

Well, there are
no _real_ winners in
a fight – are there?

tim gets the showbiz bug

Tim the Tiny Horse was <u>so</u>
small that the blacksmith
had to make his shoes from
paperclips.

His saddle was made from
a watch-strap.

Which is why he never
wore it. Well, would you?

He was small... but he
had Standards.

Most of his activities were
severely restricted. So he
spent much of his time lazing
in the sun.

Or watching the T.V.

One day Tim the Tiny Horse sat on the patio watching the ants going about their business...

He admired their
sense of purpose.

"I need to get a Job,"
he thought.

That lunchtime, as Tim sat
watching Anna Ford...

On the One O'Clock
News from the BBC,

he realised that
everyone on T.V. was
small... just like him.

It was perfect
for him!

Maybe he could be in a
cowboy film...

or the Horse of the Year
Show...

or even read the Lunchtime
News with Anna!

Maybe he'd meet that
Special Lady horse
he'd always been looking for.

He knew he shouldn't get
his hopes up as from
what he'd seen, most
of the shows on T.V.
were set in pubs...

and he didn't like
pubs because often
there was a dog in
there.

If There was one
thing Tim didn't like
it was **DOGS**.

Likes	Dislikes
Anna Ford	Dogs
Hula Hoops
sweets
FLy

Without further ado
Tim the Tiny Horse
set off for the T.V. studio.

When he arrived at the studio
everything was much bigger than
he'd been led to believe.
In fact, everything was pretty
much full size.

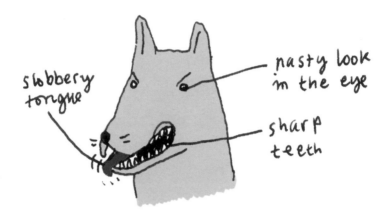

slobbery
tongue

nasty look
in the eye

sharp
teeth

Including the dog.

"I'm not sure I want to be a part of this," he thought.

And instead headed off to the canteen...

for a sugar lump.

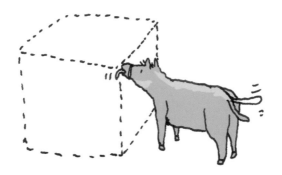

"Hmm..." thought Tim the Tiny Horse.
"The studios may not be what
I'd hoped... but the food
is first rate."

with that, he headed for home.

After all...

there's no point in
getting a job for the
sake of it.

fly gets a girlfriend

Tim the Tiny Horse
was <u>tiny</u>.

He was so small that a pizza leaflet
would take him an hour and a half
to read...

So small was Tim that even the small pizza was too big for him.

What a waste of an hour and a half.

slurp! slurp!

No. A typical lunch
for Tim the Tiny Horse
was a Hula Hoop
(preferably barbecue beef).

One day Tim's best friend Fly
announced that he had met
a lady fly and that she was
now his 'girlfriend'.

The upshot of this was that Fly
didn't want to see Tim as much.

on a couple of occasions
Tim went round
to see if Fly wanted
to come out to play,
only to find that

Fly's girlfriend was
already there.

"What does he want?"

"Perhaps she would like
to play too,"
said Tim the Tiny Horse,
hopefully.

"I think not!" said Fly's new girlfriend, looking at Tim in a way that didn't make him feel particularly welcome.

Tail drooping

Head
held
Low

Forlorn
expression

Fly explained to Tim
(over the phone) that they
could still play together

but Tim should
give a little warning
before calling round.

A short time after that, Fly's
girlfriend decided she didn't
want to see Fly any more
(although they could still be
friends).

There were no other
flies involved.

Whilst Tim was sorry to see fly so upset...

he was secretly pleased that things were back to normal.

Tim felt a little bit guilty
about this feeling...

then he remembered
the look that fly's
ex-girlfriend had given him...

and the feeling passed.

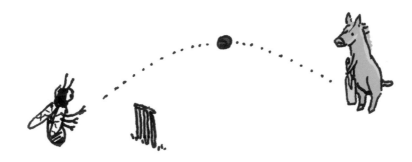

After all, you've got to stick by friends.

tim has a brush with Anna Ford

Tim the Tiny Horse was _extremely_ small.

In fact, he was so small that he found it difficult to get served in bars.

Fortunately he had
a very loud voice.

N.B.
He didn't always say 'neigh'
but when he did he meant it.

Tim mainly drank shorts.

Flashback to earlier...

Likes
Anna Ford
Hula Hoops
Sweets
Fly

Dislikes
Dogs
Fly's girlfriend

It has been established, I think, that Tim the Tiny Horse was a great fan of the BBC News at One O'Clock... with Anna Ford.

He was fascinated by Anna
and if ever a photograph of
her appeared in the newspaper...

he would cut it out and stick
it in his scrapbook.

Once, he wrote to Anna Ford
for her autograph.

After many weeks a lovely photo
of Anna arrived, signed:
"To Tim, Good LUCK, Anna Ford".

Tim the Tiny Horse pasted it on
to his bedroom wall.
He called it his Anna Ford MURAL.

Tim wrote back to Anna
asking whether it would
be possible for the two
of them to meet up.

A polite letter of refusal
came back by return of
post. It had been written
not by Anna, but by somebody
who worked with her.

For :TWO WEEKS: Tim
watched the lunchtime
news at 12.30 on ITV.

Then he went back to Anna.
Well, it doesn't do to
bear a grudge, does it?

tim and fly go out

Tim the Tiny Horse
was... well...
...very small.

To Tim a conker was a major
obstacle...

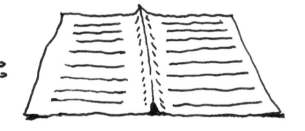

a crinkle in a piece of paper
was a real hurdle.

One day Tim and his friend
Fly decided to go to town.

They set off with Fly
riding on Tim's back.

"What an adventure!"
thought Tim the Tiny Horse.
"I could buy a <u>chair</u>!"

"And I could buy some
shoes!" said Fly
out loud.

Then Tim remembered
that most chairs were
far too big for him...

...and Fly remembered that
most shoes come in sets of
2 rather than **6**.

"Is this trip entirely necessary?"
Said Tim the Tiny Horse.
"After all, we don't really
need anything from town."

"Yes," said Fly, "and the town
is an awfully long way."

The answer was obvious:

With that they headed home.
This time it was Tim's turn to
ride on the back of Fly.

Sometimes you're
better off just staying
<u>IN</u>

tim and fly consider the meaning of life

Tim the Tiny Horse and his
best friend Fly were in
the park, staring at the
clouds and chatting.

"I wonder if there
is such a thing as
GOD," said Fly.

"I should think so,"
said Tim the Tiny Horse.

"What about all the
bad things that happen
in the world...?"

"Like war, earthquakes and famine?" said Fly.

"Well, we've all done things
we're not proud of,"
said Tim.

And he started to
think about a grape he'd
eaten off the floor of the
supermarket without paying
for it.

At that point the sun
came out.

"Draw your own conclusion
from that!" he said,
pointing at the sky.

Fly looked
rather sheepish.

Sometimes you have to see
the bigger picture.

tim the tiny horse logs on

Tim the Tiny Horse
was exceedingly small.

In fact, given a cocktail stick,
a piece of cotton and a hawthorn
berry...

Tim could play swing ball.

lolly stick

saw here

[Having formed a bat from
a discarded lolly stick]

Tim often played his best
friend Fly at swing ball...

but rarely won as Fly would
often play the ball high.

Fly had been going on
about how his sister
had been learning at
school about the
internet...

and how fantastic
it was.

" You can look up
anything you want
and find out all
about it, "
said Fly.

so One day Tim the Tiny Horse trotted off to the Internet Café to log on.

However, when he got there ...

He couldn't think of
anything to look up.

so he looked himself up.

The internet then told him
all about a tortoise called
Tim who lived to be a hundred
and sixty years old,

but was now dead.

Tim thought about
what it would be
like to be **160**
and shuddered.

As he trotted home he thought
about his experience at the
Internet Café...

and resented the way
the internet had made him
think about something he
hadn't really wanted to
confront yet.

Ageing... and his own
mortality.

on top of that, when he
arrived home there was a
note on Tim's door from Fly,

saying that he'd called round
to see if Tim wanted to play
but Tim had been out.

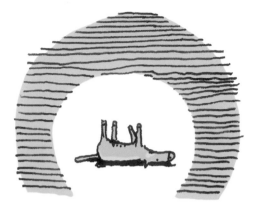

It seemed the internet
wasn't as fantastic as
Tim had been led to
believe.

Author's Note: Tim always lies on his back
when particularly frustrated.

tim does
some cooking

Tim the Tiny Horse was by
no means a large horse...

but what he lacked
in the stature department
he more than made up for
in enthusiasm.

For instance, Tim was far too
small to take part in the
London Marathon...

[all those pounding feet
would pose a real danger
to him]

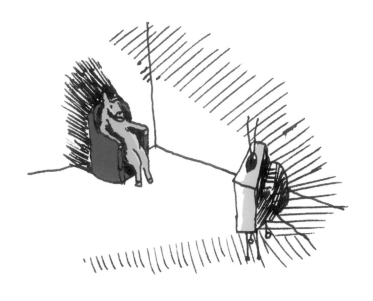

but that didn't stop him
enjoying it on the television.

One day, Tim the Tiny Horse
came upon the discarded wrapper
of a FUDGE BAR!

On closer inspection Tim realised
that there was a list of ingredients.

"The fools!"
thought Tim the Tiny Horse.
"There's nothing to stop people
from making their own fudge bars!"

Back in his kitchen he set about
making his first fudge bar.

"Let's see what I need," he said, reading the list of ingredients. "Sugar... I've got that..."

"chocolate... I've got that ... "

"But what is 'non-hydrogenated vegetable fat?'"

"Hmmm," he thought.

"Best leave it to the experts."

And he ate the sugar...

and the chocolate...

and with a little imagination
it tasted a bit like
...fudge!

tim goes
for a job
in radio

Tim the Tiny Horse was,
I'm afraid to say, a little
on the sm_all_ side.

If, for instance, he was to eat
a whole Malteser...
it might take him a whole morning.
                    AND...

he would get a Headache
and have to spend the afternoon
in BED.

A tube of toothpaste
would last him...

well, he'd had
the same tube
for **3** years...

and there was still only a
slight dent in it.

Tim was small...
but ambitious.

One afternoon, after the News at One O'Clock with Anna Ford, Tim sat listening to the cricket on the radio.

Suddenly it dawned on him.

"Radio would be perfect
for me!" he said
out loud.

"On radio it's all in the voice.
It doesn't matter how big
you are!"

His best friend Fly told him
that what he needed to do
was make a 'demo' tape of
his voice and send it to the
people who ran the radio.

'demo', it seems, was short for
demonstration.

Tim unearthed an old tape recorder.

"I'll be the producer," said Fly and pressed the record button.

" um... er... "

Unfortunately, when put on the spot, Tim the Tiny Horse couldn't think of anything to say.

"UM...I..."

"......hello."

All he could manage
was 'hello'.

To spare Tim any embarrassment
Fly told him there was a
'technical fault' with the tape.

They agreed that radio was
much harder than it looked.

Much easier just to
listen to it.

tim finds out that he is a winner

Tim the Tiny Horse was not just <u>small</u> but, well, <u>tiny</u>. (As they say, there's a clue in the name.)

He was so small he would use a bottle-top as a hot-tub.

He had to use a cotton bud to scrub his back.

One night, just after running his bath, the phone rang.

It was a strange man
who told Tim that he had
won a prize.

The man explained
that Tim may have
won a car, a holiday
or cash.

Immediately Tim's mind
began to race.

Clearly a car was
no good to him,

as his feet wouldn't be able
to reach the pedals...

Even if it was the car, he could always sell it and take the cash.

But a holiday, or money...

The strange man went on
to explain that, in fact, Tim
had not won the prize **yet**

but he would be put
into a prize draw.

This scared Tim
as he had once
become trapped in
a chest of drawers
as a foal.

At this point Tim looked
over at the lovely hot
steaming bath...

If he left it
much longer it
would start to
get cold.

"I think I'll give it a miss,"
said Tim the Tiny Horse
to the strange man.
   "But good luck with it!"

Moments later Tim was having
a lovely warm soak.

" Why do they always phone
at bath time ? "
he wondered.

tim faces up
to reality

I think we're beginning to get
the idea that in the SIZE stakes
Tim the Tiny Horse had very
little to offer.

No, he had other strengths:

Optimism...

enthusiasm...

and an interest
in current affairs...

hmm...

particularly when presented by Anna Ford.

One night, Tim the Tiny Horse and his best friend Fly sat watching a television programme...

in which there were
a number of hidden
cameras...

spying on people
living in a house.

Not a lot happened.

Fly explained
to Tim that this
was called Reality T.V.

"Reality T.V. would
be perfect for me!"
said Tim the Tiny Horse...

and raced towards
a dwarf cupboard...

in search of his
camcorder.

Tim set up the camcorder in his front room ...

and filmed...

everything...

he did...

the next day.

That evening Tim the Tiny Horse
played his reality T.V. show
to Fly,

who fell asleep
after 5 minutes.

" Hmmm..."
thought Tim the
Tiny Horse.

YAWN

"I think this show
Should be about
4 minutes long."

Sometimes **REALITY** is better in small doses.

tim's
christmas

christmas was always
a bit quiet for Tim
- being an orphan...

... and not being a particularly big fan of The Vicar of Dibley.

[Although loving Dawn French in lots of other things]

Fly, on the other hand,
spent Christmas with
his family.

Also, Anna Ford tended
to have the day off
which just added to
Tim's sense of isolation.

At Christmas Tim the Tiny Horse cooked a chicken nugget which he ate part of hot for Lunch...

then the rest cold over
the next few days.

pudding was
a fruit pastille.

This year Fly had given
Tim a Christmas cracker.

"A fat lot of good that is!"
thought Tim the Tiny Horse,
Looking at the cracker.

Then Tim had an Idea.

He wedged one end of the cracker
in the doorway and pulled...

and pulled...

and pulled.

Until the cracker
snapped.

unfortunately, the door had won.

Tim the Tiny Horse
was now in a quandary.

Should he take the door's
winnings?

" I'll take the toy
but leave the Joke
and hat,"
he thought.

That seemed fair.

The toy was a green
plastic horse.

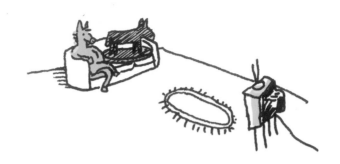

Tim the Tiny Horse sat on the
sofa with the green plastic
horse and watched...

The Vicar of Dibley.

And for a moment
Tim had an idea of what it
would be like to have a Mummy.

(And, on top of that, Dawn French reminded
him of a slightly fuller Anna Ford.)